Fairy Ponies

Magic Necklace

Zanna Davidson

Illustrated by Barbara Bongini

Meet the Ponies

Holly

Puck

Bluebell

Pony Queen

Princess Rosabel

Spray

Unicorn Prince

Izagard

Shadow

Contents

Chapter One

Holly stood beneath the swaying branches of the oak tree at the bottom of her great-aunt's garden. Under the full moon, the tree had taken on a silvery glow.

Holly glanced around to make sure no one was watching, then slipped her hand into her pocket and pulled out a tiny bag of magic dust. It felt light as gossamer in her palm.

She undid the clasp and gazed at the dust, sparkling in the moonlight. *One pinch of this,* she thought, *and I'll be fairy-sized — small enough to enter Pony Island.*

Holly had never dreamed her stay with Great-Aunt May would turn into such an adventure. She had discovered that inside the oak tree was a secret, magical land full of fairy ponies. They had welcomed her into their world and given her a bag of sparkling magic dust and a tiny silver bell, so she could visit them whenever she wanted.

Holly closed her eyes and sprinkled herself with magic dust. As soon as the dust touched her skin, she felt a tingling, shrinking feeling. Musical notes chimed in her ears, and when she opened her eyes, she realized with a gasp that she really was fairy-sized.

The oak tree now towered above her, its roots the size of branches where they writhed above the ground, the hole between them now looking like a huge, dark tunnel. Holly trembled with excitement as she whispered the spell the Pony Queen had taught her:

"Let me pass into the magic tree,
Where fairy ponies fly wild and free.
Show me the trail of sparkling light,
To Pony Island, shining bright."

She reached for the delicate silver necklace the Pony Queen had given her, and rang its tiny silver bell. A magical sound floated down the tunnel. Holly knew it would ring out through Pony Island, letting her friend Puck know she was on her way.

As she walked down the tunnel, Holly saw a trail of diamond-bright light, guiding her

through the darkness. The tunnel twisted and
turned, this way and that,
and as she rounded a
corner, Holly gave
a cry of delight.
There was Pony
Island! It was
only the second
time she had seen it, and it was just as
beautiful as she remembered.

Holly ran the rest of the way, bursting out
into a sun-filled meadow, thick with
butterflies and wild flowers. She loved the feel
of the lush green grass between her toes.

There was a sound of beating wings, and
Holly looked up to see Puck swooping
through the sky, his delicate butterfly wings

glinting in the sunlight, his glossy coat the russet-brown of autumn leaves.

"Holly!" he cried, pirouetting through the air in excitement.

He landed gracefully beside her, his hoofs barely making a sound on the soft earth.

"I'm so glad you're back," he said. "And," he went on eagerly, "the Pony Queen wants to see you again, too. She asked me to bring you to her as soon as you arrived. She's going to take us on a tour of the Summer Palace."

"Wow!" Holly beamed. "That sounds amazing…"

Puck bent his knees, so Holly could swing herself up by his mane. The next moment, he was pushing off with his hind legs and fluttering his gossamer wings. They rose up and up, into the cloudless sky.

Holly wrapped her arms around Puck's neck, pressing her body close to his for comfort, trying not to think of the ground rapidly disappearing below them. Puck seemed to have forgotten Holly wasn't used to flying as he swooped and dived over treetops, zinging his way between branches.

"Look down, Holly," Puck told her. "You'll
see more of Pony Island! We're flying over the
Magic Pony Pools now."

Holly finally allowed herself to look and
saw a sparkling lake full of ponies prancing
through the water. Their pretty wings
shimmered like pieces of a rainbow.

As they glided above its smooth surface,
Holly caught sight of their reflection in the
water.

"Look – there we are!" she cried. "I can see
us flying. I'm *really* flying!"

Holly felt giddy with excitement, but she wasn't afraid any more. Puck's silky smooth coat was soft beneath her fingertips, and it was amazing to pass over treetops and look down on the magical world below. She could see the wild flower meadows by the Great Oak, and beyond it, a beautiful valley, alive with butterflies. A warm breeze washed over her as they flew and she felt free as a bird, light as air.

"You haven't seen anything yet!" said Puck. "Just wait until we get to the palace."

Holly smiled at the thought, then tilted her head as she caught the faint strains of a few chiming notes.

"Can you hear that sound?" she asked. "What is it?"

"It's the Singing River," Puck explained. "It'll come into view soon."

They followed the river as it wound its way through grassy fields. The further they flew, the more notes filled the air, coming together to make a lilting melody that rose from the river like a silver ribbon of sound.

As they rounded the corner, Holly had her first view of the Summer Palace. It stood on the banks of the Singing River, its curved turrets reaching up into the sky. Its walls were made of marble, white and gleaming in the sunlight. The front was laced with climbing roses, which arched above the doorway.

Puck swooped down to land on the path beside the palace, just as the Pony Queen came out to greet them.

She moved so gracefully, it was almost as if she were floating. Her shimmering wings fluttered gently, filling the air with sparkles. On her head, she wore a delicate crown of flowers, and a halo of golden dust glittered all around her.

"Welcome, Holly," she said, in her musical voice.

Holly was about to reply, but before she could say anything, there was a sudden rush of wind and a great black pony with large gleaming wings, raced out of the palace.

"What is it, Shadow?" asked the Pony Queen, seeing his anxious face.

"It's the Necklace of Wishes," cried Shadow. "It's been stolen!"

Chapter Two

"No!" gasped the Pony Queen. "How can that be?"

"I've just spoken with Storm and Ravenstar, the palace guards," Shadow went on, his voice low and urgent. "They saw a mystery pony escaping from the palace. Storm and Ravenstar tried to follow him, but he managed to lose them. They think he's

heading for Rainbow Shore. We'll need the
most powerful ponies in the kingdom to catch
him."

"I'll call for the Spell-Keepers," announced
the Pony Queen, taking to the air, and flying
up to the topmost turret.

Shielding her eyes against the sun, Holly
watched as the Pony Queen rang a large

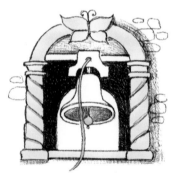
silver bell that hung
from the turret. It sent
a ringing peal through
the air. The Pony
Queen fluttered back
down to the ground and, moments later,
ponies came from all directions, flying faster
than the wind as they raced towards the
palace. There were bays and roans, black

ponies and palominos, each with shimmering, butterfly wings. Among them, Holly recognized Bluebell, Puck's mother, with her dapple grey coat and long flowing mane, and his uncle, Dancer. The ponies began a whispered discussion and Holly looked at the ponies' horrified faces as they heard the news.

"We'll leave right away for Rainbow Shore," the Pony Queen told Shadow. "I'm sorry not to show you around the palace today, Holly," she added. "Another time…"

"You two stay behind," warned Bluebell. "I know you love adventure, Puck, but this could be dangerous. Take Holly back to our house. There's fresh dewberry cordial and honey cakes waiting for you."

"Thank you," Holly called, as Bluebell

soared into the sky with the other Spell-
Keepers, following the Pony Queen's lead.

Holly couldn't believe how fast they flew.
One moment the ponies were above the
palace, the next they were flying in
a line across the sky,

their tails streaming behind them.

"I wish I were a Spell-Keeper," said Puck wistfully.

"Then we could go with them and help find the necklace. They always have the best adventures."

"Who are they?" asked Holly.

"The most magical and important ponies on the island," Puck replied. "They've spent years training in magic. They help the Pony Queen protect Pony Island."

As he spoke, Puck looked around and saw Shadow cantering back to the palace.

"Why didn't Shadow go with the others?" asked Holly.

"He's Captain of the Palace Guards, not a Spell-Keeper," Puck explained. "He wanted to be, but I suppose the Pony Queen didn't think his magic was strong enough... I know!" he cried suddenly, a mischievous twinkle in his eye. "Let's go into the palace and look for clues ourselves."

"Shouldn't we go back to your house, like your mother said?" asked Holly.

"It can't do any harm, looking around the palace," said Puck,

He turned around to look pleadingly at Holly.

"Okay," she said at last. "But only for a
moment."

"I can't believe someone's actually stolen
the Necklace of Wishes," Puck went on.
"Every pony goes to see it in their first year
at Pony Magic School. It's always been kept

at the palace, in a tiny room filled with roses. Come on, I'll show you!"

As they entered the palace, Holly looked around in wide-eyed wonder. She was in a spacious courtyard, filled with flowers. The soothing sound of falling water came from four marble fountains, and looking up, Holly could see slender trees, their entwined branches forming a vast domed ceiling. Sunlight filtered through the leaves, flooding the courtyard with a magical and watery-green light.

"It's beautiful," whispered Holly.

Looking around for Puck, she realized he was already heading out of the courtyard, through a narrow archway that led deeper into the palace. Holly had to run quickly to catch up with him.

"What does the necklace look like?" she asked, filled with curiosity.

Puck's eyes lit up as he began to describe it. "It's made of precious jewels and has the power to grant a wish to whoever wears it," he said. "But each time a wish is made, its powers diminish. That's why we keep it so closely guarded. It's only meant to be used in times of great emergency. It's one of the oldest and most treasured pieces of Pony Magic."

Puck's hoofs echoed on the smooth marble floor as they walked down the palace's long corridors. Holly glimpsed rooms lined with ancient spell books and others filled with magical treasures.

"Seashells from Rainbow Shore," said Puck,
as they walked past a room bursting with
hundreds of shells.

"And I can smell flowers," said Holly,
breathing in a rush of sweet air. "It's like
being in a summer meadow."

"Look in the next room," said Puck. "It's
filled with flowers from the Forever Flower

Meadows. Their scent fills the palace."

"Look!" said Holly suddenly, pointing straight ahead at an intricately carved wooden door, nestled in an archway at the end of the corridor.

"That's it!" cried Puck, galloping towards it. "That's the room where the necklace was kept!"

Carved into the door itself was a poem,

written in elegant, sloping writing.

I am the Necklace of Wishes, burning bright,
See my jewels, shining like starlight.
But more precious still is my magic power,
To grant you whatever you most desire.

"Reading that almost makes me want the necklace for myself," said Puck.

He gently nudged open the door and they entered the room. Holly caught a brief glimpse of a beautiful rose bower and petals scattered across the floor, when the sound of hoofs made her look up. There was a flash of a long, dark tail as it disappeared behind a door on the opposite side of the room, then the door slammed shut with a bang.

Chapter Three

"Who was that?" Holly wondered aloud.

"I don't know – but we're going to find out," Puck declared.

They raced across the room and through the other door, but the mystery pony was nowhere to be seen. In the silence of the palace, Holly and Puck could just make out the sound of muffled hoof beats, cantering away.

"Why are they running away?" asked Holly. "Unless – do you think it could be the thief, or one of his gang?"

"But that doesn't make any sense," said Puck. "Come on, jump on my back, Holly. There's only one way to find out."

Puck crouched down, and Holly swung herself up in one swift movement. Then Puck galloped after the hoof beats, picking up speed fast. They just caught a glimpse of a black tail slipping around a corner ahead of

them, but as they came out into the palace gardens, the pony had disappeared.

"We've lost him!" cried Puck, his voice full of anguish.

Holly gazed up at the sky to see if the pony had flown away, but there was no sign of him.

"He can't have just disappeared," she said, trying to work things out. She glanced around, but couldn't see anywhere for the pony to hide. "Where do the gardens lead?" she asked.

"To the Singing River," said Puck. "Quick!"

Puck leaped forward so fast, Holly had to grab hold of his mane to stay on. But when they reached the water, all that was left were a few ripples and a stream of bubbles, rising to the surface.

"Look!" said Puck, pointing to the bubbles.

"I think he must have escaped into the river."

"Can we follow him?" asked Holly.

Puck shook his head, sorrowfully. "We need an invitation from a river pony. Adult ponies can enter the river, but younger ponies have to ask permission. I'd have to summon a river pony first and ask."

"Then summon a river pony!" said Holly, eagerly.

"Umm…" Puck replied, his voice glum. "You need to whistle a special tune. We were taught it at Pony Magic School…but I can never remember it!"

Puck and Holly stood for a moment, gazing down at the bubbling water, thinking of the mystery pony, slipping further from their grasp.

"We can't stop here," said Holly. "Not when we're this close. Try the whistle – just see if you can do it."

As she spoke, she slid off his back and stepped away from him, trying to give him space to remember.

"Okay," said Puck, his eyes closed in thought. Then he let out a series of long, flute-like whistles.

Puck and Holly waited, staring at the crystal waters. Nothing happened.

"Maybe the whistles go up at the end?" Puck said, frowning as he tried to remember the tune. This time he bent low over the river, changing the melody. But the waters still refused to part.

"I know! I know!" cried Puck. "The first whistle goes up at the end, then after that they stay low."

Puck spent the next few minutes trying every tune he could think of. Holly was about to suggest they give up when the water began bubbling and gurgling, and a young river pony rose above the surface on four glittering dragonfly wings. His body shimmered pearly green and his eyes were ocean-blue.

"Greetings!" he said with a grin, "I'm Spray. Wow," he added, "you must be Holly. I've heard about you. Welcome to Pony Island!"

He turned to look at Puck.

"That's some of the worst whistling I've ever heard," he added.

Holly saw Puck's brow frown with anger, and quickly stepped in.

"Please," she said, "we need your help. This is my friend, Puck. We're looking for the Necklace of Wishes. We were following a pony who we suspect might have something to do with its disappearance. We think he dived into the Singing River."

"If I sprinkle you with coral dust, you can enter the river and follow him," said Spray. "But there's one condition…"

"What's that?" asked Puck.

"That I can come too. I want to help find the necklace. I love adventure!"

"Of course you can come," said Puck,

grinning back at him.

Spray lost no time. He fluttered over to where they were standing and hovered above them, vigorously flapping his wings. A moment later, he was showering them with a sparkling dust.

"Now the coral dust has touched your skin, you can breathe underwater," Spray explained. "Follow me!"

He turned and dived effortlessly back into the water.

"Hold on tight!" said Puck.

Holly gripped his mane, closed her eyes and together they plunged deep into the water.

Chapter Four

Down, down, down they went, following
Spray's beating tail as he dived towards the
riverbed. All around them the water was crystal
clear and Holly could see shimmering fish
flashing before her. She put her arms around
Puck's neck and hugged his body so he could
swim faster. Puck beat his wings and kicked his
legs, powering them through the water.

"It's like a whole new magical world," said Holly, amazed her voice sounded as clear underwater as it did in the air.

Spray stopped when he reached the bottom, which was covered in fine, soft sand. Puck came to a halt beside him. Ahead, Holly could see twisting, curving houses rising out of the riverbed, carved out of pale-blue coral. Glistening water plants grew in the crevices, their fronds waving in the warm current.

"Where do you think we should look first?" Holly asked Spray. "There's no sign of the mystery pony here."

"Perhaps he's gone somewhere to hide," said Spray, "somewhere secret, far away from the other ponies…" He paused for a moment, deep in thought.

Meanwhile, Puck's eyes shone with excitement.

"I know where we should go!" he cried. "The Tangled Forest… It's a hidden underwater forest – Dandelion told me about it. We've never been, but it's one of the most secret places on the island."

"The Tangled Forest!" repeated Spray.

"I'm not sure we should go there."

"What is the Tangled Forest?" asked Holly. There was something about the way they said its name that made her feel wary.

"It's one of the oldest, creepiest, darkest places on Pony Island," Puck explained with relish. "Full of strange plants and slimy, slippery water creatures."

"Exactly!" said Spray. "I don't think we should risk it."

"Oh come on," said Puck. "I thought you said you loved adventure? It sounds like the perfect hideout for a pony thief."

"I like *little* adventures," said Spray, backing away. "Not great big scary get-lost-in-the-Tangled-Forest adventures."

Puck looked at Holly, his eyes begging her to persuade Spray.

"We'll need you as our guide to get there," said Holly, gently. "Please help us. It's so important we find that necklace. If we don't, the pony thief might use its powers and who knows what bad things he might wish for."

"Okay," said Spray at last, tossing his mane determinedly. "This way."

Puck whinnied with excitement and plunged after him. Holly knew there was no going back now. She gulped nervously, trying to quell the fluttering feeling inside her tummy.

The further they swam away from the little houses, the colder and darker the water became. The underwater plants began to grow more thickly, so that their leafy fronds brushed her body as they moved between them. Ahead, Holly could see a dense maze of plants, tightly packed together and swaying in the current. Holly slid off Puck's back and swam behind him to avoid the leafy tendrils. As the water grew darker, Puck, Spray and Holly swam closer together, their eyes darting from left to right.

"We're in the Tangled Forest now, aren't

we?" asked Holly, dropping her voice to a hushed whisper.

Puck simply nodded in reply. Holly realized he was feeling just as scared as she was. Soon it was so dark, Holly could only just see Spray in front of them — beyond that the world became a murky gloom. Everything was eerily quiet, except for a strange rushing sound, as if something was moving slowly along beside them in the water.

Stop it! Holly told herself. *You're just imagining things.*

But at that moment she felt something cold and slimy curl around her ankle, gripping hold of her tightly.

"Help!" she cried.

Spray and Puck whipped around to look.

"Oh no!" screamed Spray. "It's the riversnatchers!"

"Wh-wh-what are they?" asked Holly. "I can't get it off me! Oh yuck! Its suckers are sticking to me..."

"I didn't realize the riversnatchers were real!" said Spray. "My parents told me about them, but I thought they were just trying to stop me from going into the forest."

"Well, this one feels pretty real,"

said Holly, as its tentacles grabbed her leg.
She kicked out, desperately trying to free
herself, but the more Holly struggled, the
tighter the creature gripped her.

"HELP!" she cried. "It won't let me go."

"And there's more of them coming," added Puck.

Looking up, they saw the water was thick with riversnatchers drifting towards them, their long, arm-like tentacles reaching out.

"Swim!" cried Spray. "As fast as you can!"

But it was too late. Every way they went they were surrounded by the slimy, slippery riversnatchers.

"I can't move!" said Holly.

"Stop struggling!" said Spray. He had been twisting and turning in the water, trying to escape, but suddenly he stood stock-still. "The more you struggle, the tighter the grip becomes."

"That doesn't really help us," said Puck. "Can't you remember any other ways to escape them?"

As he spoke, Puck began trying to free Holly, snapping at the riversnatchers that were winding around her.

"It's no use," said Spray, staring in horror at the army of enchanted creatures. "We're trapped!"

Chapter Five

"Okay, let's keep calm," said Holly, thinking hard. "And let's stay as still as we can. It only gets worse when we move. There must be a way out of this."

Puck gulped. "Not that I can think of."

"Isn't there some magic that can help us?" asked Holly.

"We could try a freezing spell," suggested

Puck, desperation in his voice. "At least that would stop the riversnatchers in their tracks, and give us time to escape."

"Okay!" cried Holly. "Quick – say one!"

"Um…I don't actually know one," said Puck.

"Nor do I," added Spray, glumly.

"Then let's just make up a spell to send them away," suggested Holly, her voice shaky with panic. "Can you do that?"

"We can try," said Spray.

Puck furrowed his brow in thought. "It might work. The spell must be in rhyme, that's the key. Let's see…

Riversnatchers, riversnatchers, one, two, three,
Hear my words and set us free!"

Nothing happened.

"I'm not surprised that didn't work," grumbled Spray. "That spell was about as bad as your whistling."

"Fine!" snapped Puck. "You try."

Spray was silent for a long time. As the seconds ticked by, Holly could see more and more riversnatchers gliding through the water towards them. She realized with fear that their slimy tentacles were now wrapped around her entire body. She couldn't even move her fingers.

"Anything, Spray?" Holly asked breathlessly.

"I'm trying!" said Spray. "It's hard to make up a spell on the spot. I know! I'll try one I've already learned. It's meant to ward off river sprites, but if I change the words, it might work on riversnatchers too."

Spray began gabbling the spell as fast as he could.

"By the power of the river, the rushes and reeds,

I cast a spell to meet my needs –

Whip up the waters, make their waves strong,

And send the snatchers back where they belong."

Even as he finished speaking, Holly could feel the water around her start to swirl and swell. The riversnatchers trailing towards them were whipped away by the surging current and those that had only just started to take hold were sucked back as well. "Brilliant!" cried Puck. "It's working."

"It is!" agreed Spray, as the waves grew stronger. "I've never actually used this spell before. I just read it in a spell book…"

"What about the whipping waters, Spray?" interrupted Holly, as she was buffeted this way and that by the waves. "What are they going to do to us?"

"Oh!" said Spray. "Um…I'm not really sure about that."

The waves were growing stronger all the time. One by one, the riversnatchers were plucked by the frenzied water and carried away. Holly could move her arms and legs now, but she soon began to tumble around in the water, somersaulting over and over in the whirling current. She gripped onto Puck, pulling herself up onto his back.

"Make it stop!" shouted Holly.

Spray shook his head. "I don't know the spell for that," he shouted back.

"Hold tight, Holly," said Puck.

The next moment there was a rush of water and Holly felt herself being hurtled along. She clung onto Puck as they were pushed through the Tangled Forest. Behind her, she could just make out Spray in the swirling water as he was dragged along with them.

The water pounded in her ears and she felt as if she were on an underwater roller coaster that would never end. As the plants in the forest flashed past her, she could feel her grip loosening on Puck.

"Keep hold of me, Holly!" cried Puck, feeling her fingers slide from his mane. "I don't want to lose you."

"I'm trying," panted Holly, as another burst of water whooshed against her side.

Holly looked around the dark forest, with its thickly tangled plants, and wondered how she'd ever find Puck again if they were separated.

Teeth gritted, she tried to grip onto Puck's mane, but at that moment the current surged between them. Holly was flung to one side and tumbled around until she didn't know which way was up.

"Puck!" she cried. But he was nowhere to be seen.

She was lost and alone in the underwater forest.

Chapter Six

Over and over Holly tumbled, too dizzy to
think. She had no idea where she was now, nor
how long the storm would last.

Suddenly, the water was flooded with light,
and with one final whoosh, the current jetted
her out of the forest, into calm waters once
more. Holly gasped with relief. She tried to
swim forward, but her head was still spinning

and she could only stumble along the sandy
riverbed, trying to regain her balance. A
moment later, there was a rush of water, and
Puck landed beside her.

"Oh Holly!" he cried. "I thought I'd never
see you again. I'm so glad I've found you."

"Me too," said Holly, hugging him tightly.

A few seconds later, something large and

heavy crashed into them both. It was Spray, his legs shaking, his face pale.

"I'm…sorry," he said, panting for breath. "The…spell…didn't work…quite the way I expected."

"That water ride was definitely an adventure," said Puck, his legs still wobbly as jelly.

"An adventure?" said Spray. "If that was an adventure then I never want one again."

Puck laughed, unable to believe Spray meant it. "We're still no closer to finding the mystery pony though," he said, suddenly downcast. "Or the necklace."

"We did our best, Puck," replied Holly, trying to comfort him. "I think it's time we left the river, though. The Pony Queen might be back at the Summer Palace by now. We should go and tell her what we saw."

"Okay," agreed Puck sadly. "Let's head to the Dancing Waterfall. I know a shortcut to the Palace from there."

"Thank you, Spray," said Holly, giving the river pony a hug.

"At least now I know what the Tangled Forest is like," Puck added with a grin.

"Goodbye," Holly called, as she climbed onto Puck's back. Puck kicked off with his hind legs and beat his wings as fast as he could, powering them up through the water to the Dancing Waterfall.

Soon they broke the surface, shooting out in a blur of glistening wings and sparkling water droplets. Holly was glad to breathe in the fresh, clear air once more. Looking around, she saw that they were in a little secret cove, with a sandy bay, tucked away behind the waterfall.

Puck fluttered down to the sand, and Holly slipped off his back, shivering in her wet clothes.

"Cold?" Puck asked.

Holly nodded, trying to keep her teeth from chattering.

"Well, at least there's a spell I *do* know," said Puck.

"Blow, warm air, blow,
Gentle and slow
Caress our skin dry
As you breeze by..."

"Lovely!" cried Holly, as warm wind swept over them both, drying Holly's clothes in seconds.

She shook her hair and watched as the last water drops magically disappeared.

"We always say that spell after washing at the Magic Pony P—"

"Shh!" interrupted Holly with a whisper. "Can you hear that sound? It's coming from the tunnel in the rock."

Holly and Puck held their breath as they heard the faint echoes of voices.

"I can't hear what they're saying," she said, "they're too far away. Shall we see who it is?"

Puck nodded, his eyes alight with excitement. "It could be the mystery pony!"

The tunnel was too low for Holly to ride on

Puck, so she crept along behind him, her heart pounding as she tiptoed across the sandy floor. They turned a corner in the tunnel and Puck stopped suddenly. Peering around him, Holly could see why. The tunnel opened out into a cave, which was lit by a flickering light, casting dancing shadows over the walls. Further tunnels stretched out from the cave, leading deeper into the rock.

"The voices are coming from the cave," whispered Puck.

They tiptoed forwards, keeping their backs pressed against the wall of the tunnel, trying to stay hidden. As more of the cave came into view, Puck let out a stifled gasp.

Standing in front of them, at the entrance to the cave, was Shadow, the Captain of the

Palace Guards. Around his neck, shimmering brightly against the darkness, was the Necklace of Wishes.

Chapter Seven

As Holly's eyes grew accustomed to the
dazzling light of the necklace, she caught
sight of two more ponies hidden in the
shadows, their eyes glinting menacingly.

"That's Storm and Ravenstar, the palace
guards," Puck hissed. "What are they doing
here?"

Holly frowned anxiously at Puck, urging

him to keep quiet. Shadow's voice grew louder now and was swelling with pride.

"This is the moment I've been waiting for!" he declared. "Finally, the Necklace of Wishes is mine! The Pony Queen has never recognized my talents – my skill, my cunning. Now she's going to realize the mistake she made when she refused to make me a Spell-Keeper."

Puck stiffened in anger and Holly shook her head, trying to stop him from rushing out.

"I can't believe it," hissed Puck. "It was Shadow who stole the necklace. Storm and Ravenstar must have been

helping him all along…"

Holly put her finger to her lips.

"Shh!" she whispered, terrified they'd be overheard. "We can't let them find us, or we'll be in more danger than ever."

Shadow let out a long, low laugh.

"I've proved how weak the Spell-Keepers really are, though," he went on. "They were too trusting. They fell for my story about the pony thief."

"What now, Shadow?" asked Ravenstar, stepping forward, so Holly could make out the bright white star on his forehead. "What are you going to wish for?"

"I'm going to take the Pony Queen's place – and rule Pony Island myself!" Shadow vowed. "I'll reward you both for your loyalty.

Storm, you helped me fool the Queen so I could steal the necklace. Ravenstar, you brought it to the secret cave. In return, I'll make you my advisors. Your first act can be to help me lock up the Pony Queen in the darkest dungeon we can find."

All three ponies began to laugh, and Holly seized the moment to whisper to Puck.

"We must do something," she said, "before it's too late. We *have* to get the necklace back from Shadow."

Puck nodded, his face full of anger at Shadow's betrayal. "I'll distract Shadow, while you grab the necklace."

"No!" said Holly. "That's too risky. Let's go and get help. Now we know where the necklace is, we should try to find the Pony Queen."

Puck looked as if he was about to agree, but their attention was caught by Shadow, who had begun speaking again.

"The time has come to make my wish."

"We have to act now!" said Puck in an urgent whisper.

Before Holly could stop him, he dashed headlong out of the tunnel and into the cave. Holly could only look on in alarm as Puck came to a stuttering halt in front of Shadow.

"Phew! I'm so glad to see you, Shadow," he said, trying to keep his voice friendly. "I'm lost. I stumbled into these caves and now I can't get out. Can you help me?"

All three ponies turned and stared in surprise at Puck. Holly realized this was her chance. She had to grab the necklace now, while the ponies were off-guard, or all would be lost.

She crept out of the tunnel and into the cave, all the while keeping in the dark. Taking a deep breath to steady her fluttering nerves, Holly leaped forward and in one swift movement grabbed hold of the necklace and pulled it over Shadow's head.

Shadow just stared at her for a moment, too shocked to move. Before he could collect himself, Holly raced over to Puck and leaped onto his back. He wheeled around, making for the cave's entrance, but Shadow blocked their way, flanked by Storm and Ravenstar.

"Not so fast, little ones," snapped Shadow. "You've got something we want."

Puck tried to circle around him again, but

Shadow reared up, bringing his hoofs crashing down in front of them. Holly had to fling her body to the side as Shadow swooped at her.

"Hurry, Puck!" she called, as Shadow lunged again, his teeth snapping the air inches from the necklace in her hand.

Puck gulped as he realized there was nothing for it – with their way back to the waterfall blocked, he had no choice but to head deeper into the caves. Galloping as hard as he could, Puck ducked into another tunnel. It was black as night, the only light coming from the magical, glittering necklace.

With the sound of pounding hoof beats close behind them, Puck was forced to take the slippery twists and turns at breakneck speed. He skidded around the craggy corners, stumbling over the sharp stones strewn across the ground.

In places the tunnel was so low, Holly had to bend right down, with her head pressed against Puck's chest, where she could hear his frantically beating heart.

The sound of the hoof beats behind them became lighter.

"We've lost one of them," cried Holly, only to realize a moment later that the pony had broken off – and was now galloping down another passageway, on the other side of the wall. "Oh no!" she said. "I think they're trying to cut us off."

Puck's breath was coming in great panting gasps. "The only thing…that can save us now…is magic."

"Can you make a spell?" asked Holly.

"Don't know one," gasped Puck. "I'll have to use the necklace. But I need to be wearing it."

Holly gripped Puck's mane with her left hand, and tried to position her other hand so she could loop the necklace around Puck's neck, but they were moving so fast she kept missing. Puck's juddering gallop forced her body up and down, up and down, so that it was all she could do to stay on.

"I must do it," she told herself through gritted teeth.

Holly gripped Puck with her legs and raised herself up, so as to get a better aim over his head. But at that moment, Puck lurched around a razor-sharp turn, throwing Holly sideways. She felt the necklace slip through her fingers and only just managed to grab hold of it again. But she'd loosened her hold on Puck. As he lurched forward, Holly felt herself sliding off him, losing her balance…

"No!" cried Holly.

At Holly's cry, Puck slowed his pace. Using all her strength, Holly hauled herself up, grasping his mane with one hand.

With the other hand, she flung the necklace
over his head.

"I've done it!" she cried. "Hurry, Puck!
Make the wish."

Puck picked up speed again, but he was so
breathless he could hardly speak.
Behind them, the hoof beats
were drawing closer.

"They're going to catch us!" Holly cried.

Ahead, she could see another small cave, with lots of passages leading off from it. Suddenly, Storm and Ravenstar appeared from hidden tunnels on either side, smiling maliciously. The chase was over. Holly and Puck were trapped.

"Necklace of Wishes, burning bright," cried Puck, his voice trembling with fear. "Take Holly and Puck to the palace tonight!"

There was a flash of light that lit the cave like a rainbow. Holly saw sparkles dance before her eyes, then felt herself being pulled backwards. She just ha d time to take in Shadow's furious face, before everything went black.

Chapter Eight

When Holly opened her eyes, she looked up to see a dappled green light above her. For a moment, she thought she was underwater again. Then she stretched her hands, taking in the soft grassy floor beneath her fingertips, the fragrant scent of wild flowers and the feel of a gentle breeze against her cheek.

"Welcome back, Holly," said a musical

voice, like the sound of tinkling bells.

"Your Majesty," gasped Holly, jumping up at the sight of the Pony Queen.

"You're in the courtyard of the Summer Palace," the Pony Queen explained, seeing her bewilderment.

"I am?" cried Holly. "So it worked, the necklace worked—" She broke off in sudden anguish. "Where's Puck? Did he make it too?"

"I'm here, Holly," said Puck, from just behind her.

Holly whipped around to see him grinning at her, the Necklace of Wishes shining brightly on his chest.

"We did it! We did it!" cried Holly.

She rushed over to Puck and hugged him. He gave a snort of delight. "I know!" he said.

"We beat Shadow and Storm and Ravenstar *and* we saved the necklace…"

A cheer went up and Holly looked around to see the Spell-Keepers gathered by the Pony Queen.

"Tell us what happened," said the Pony Queen. "We flew to Rainbow Shore, but there was no sign of the thief or the necklace. We'd just arrived back here to discuss what to do next, when you two appeared out of nowhere."

"It was Shadow who stole the necklace, he was angry at not being made a Spell-Keeper," said Puck, in a rush. "We tried to follow him, but we got trapped by the riversnatchers in the Tangled Forest—"

"You went into the Tangled Forest?" interrupted Bluebell, rushing forward. "Thank the stars you're all right," she breathed, nuzzling Puck close to her. "But you never should have gone there."

"We were fine, Mum," said Puck, already

forgetting how scary it had been. "And then we found Shadow and took the necklace back—"

"Just before he tried to overthrow the Pony Queen," finished Holly.

The Spell-Keepers gasped in shock.

"It seems Shadow has betrayed our trust," said the Pony Queen. "We must find him, even if we have to comb Pony Island from the Enchanted Wood to Rainbow Shore."

The Spell-Keepers nodded in agreement.

"But first," said the Pony Queen, "it's time to celebrate. Puck and Holly – today, you rescued the Necklace of Wishes and fought off a dangerous enemy. Such bravery deserves a reward. I'm going to hold a party for you."

And with that, the Pony Queen flew out of the palace into the gathering darkness.

Through the trees in the courtyard, Holly and Puck could see her chanting a spell. The words left her mouth to become golden writing in the sky, each letter glittering like a thousand stars.

"Fairy ponies one and all,
Come to the palace, join our ball.
Bring music so that we can sway
And with laughter, dance the night away."

"It shouldn't be long now," the Pony Queen told Puck and Holly, as she glided back into the palace. "No fairy pony can resist a party."

Holly watched in wonder as a stream of fairy ponies began flooding into the palace from every doorway and entrance. Some

carried instruments –
nutshell castanets, chiming
bluebells, harps strung with
grass and twisting shell horns.

Others came with food – delicate cakes

dusted with sparkling icing,
mounds of juicy berries
and fruit-filled tarts.

"And honeydew juice!"
cried Puck excitedly, as a fairy pony poured a
delicious mixture into petal-shaped cups.

As the great domed courtyard filled with
ponies, Puck looked longingly at the food.

"Time for a feast!" laughed the
Pony Queen, watching him.

Puck grinned at her and
began nibbling on nut

clusters soaked in honey, while Holly couldn't
resist reaching for one of the little cakes. It
melted in her mouth, light as air, while the
icing popped and fizzed on her tongue. There
were piles of peaches, plums and pears,
dewberries and blueberries, all scattered with
drops of amber sugar crystals.

As the sky grew darker, Holly could see

the stars twinkling down on them.
Fireflies wove their way between the
ponies, their bodies sparkling in the dark.
The fairy pony band began to play, while
the others danced to the music.

"Come on!" said Puck. "Climb on my
back and we'll join in."

As the fairy pony band struck up another song, the Pony Queen rose up in the middle of the courtyard, twirling in a cloud of sparkling golden dust. She looked dazzling as she danced, her graceful wings glinting under the stars. Holly felt she could have watched her for ever, but even as she looked, a great wave of tiredness washed over her, and she had to raise her hand to hide her yawn.

The Pony Queen came fluttering over to them.

"You must be tired, Holly," she said.

"You've had a day full of adventure. It's time for you to return home. You'll find little time has passed in your world while you've been here – you will still have the night ahead of you to sleep. Puck will take you back to the Great Oak," she added. "Thank you for all your help today."

Holly waved goodbye and together she and Puck took to the night skies. As they flew away from the palace, everything became quiet, except for the haunting song of the river and the occasional flutter of wings, as fairy ponies made their way home from the party.

All too soon, they reached the entrance to the Great Oak.

"Goodbye," Puck said. "Promise you'll come again soon."

"Just try to keep me away," said Holly. She stroked his silky soft muzzle, and kissed him gently on the nose, then set off once more through the tunnel.

The oak tree's smooth walls now felt familiar to her touch. As she reached the entrance to her world, she gazed out at Great-Aunt May's garden. It seemed like the garden of a giant to her fairy-sized self – a thick forest of grass and flowers. Then she pulled out the tiny leaf with rainbow writing that the Pony Queen had given her on her very first visit to Pony Island. She whispered its secret spell:

"I'm fairy Holly, I close my eyes,
Stretch my arms, reach for the skies,
Magic me back to my human size."

As she said the words, she felt her body
begin to tingle all over. Stars danced before her
eyes and when she opened them she was no
longer fairy-sized. She was a girl again,
standing next to the gnarled old oak tree.

She peered back through the tiny hole
between the roots – and saw nothing but
darkness.

"What a wonderful secret," Holly whispered
to herself. "And to think it's always there…a
magical world and another adventure, just
waiting to happen. I can't wait to go back…"

Edited by Stephanie King and Becky Walker

Designed by Brenda Cole

Reading consultant: Alison Kelly,
University of Roehampton

First published in 2014 by Usborne Publishing Ltd.,
Usborne House, 83-85 Saffron Hill, London EC1N 8RT, England.
www.usborne.com